This
MOUSE ⊞ WORKS
Classics Collection Storybook

belongs to

KRISTA

Mr. Potato Head® and Mrs. Potato Head® Playskool Rockin Robot® Playskool Nursery® Monitor,
Barrel of Monkeys® Ants in the Pants® Twister® Operation® and Candyland® are registered trademarks
of Hasbro, Inc. Used with permission. © Hasbro, Inc. All rights reserved. Slinky® Dog © James Industries.
Little Tikes® Toddle Tots® Fire Truck © The Little Tikes Company. See N' Say® Farmer Says © Mattel, Inc.
Printed in the United States of America
ISBN: 1-57082-460-6
1 3 5 7 9 10 8 6 4 2

Do you have one toy that is extra special? You know the kind. You spend hours playing with it, acting out all kinds of adventures. For a little boy named Andy, a talking cowboy doll named Woody was his favorite toy. He'd spend hours playing cowboys with Woody. Andy would turn his toys into bank robbers and frightened townspeople. But Woody was always the guy who saved the day!

When Andy pretended that Mr. Potato Head was mean ol' One-Eyed Black Bart robbing a bank, he only had to pull Woody's string. Then Woody would say, "Reach for the sky!" and Black Bart knew he was done for.

"You saved the day, Woody," Andy would yell. He'd give Woody a ride on his shoulders.

One day, Andy's mom sent him to bring his little sister Molly downstairs. Andy left Woody on his bed. Today was a big day. Today was Andy's birthday party.

7

"What do you think?" asked Andy's mom. "This looks great, Mom!" Andy answered. And it did. The room was decorated with balloons, streamers, and a great big banner that said HAPPY BIRTHDAY, ANDY!

While Andy was downstairs greeting his friends, up in his room an amazing thing was happening. Woody was coming to life, and as he did he yelled out to the rest of the toys, "Okay, everybody...the coast is clear!"

All of Andy's toys began to stir: Hamm, the piggy bank; Rex the tyrannosaurus; Woody's faithful dog, Slinky; the sweet Little Miss Bo Peep; and Mr. Potato Head.

Calling a meeting of all the toys, Woody asked them if they were prepared for the family's move the next week. "I don't want any toys left behind. A moving buddy—if you don't have one, get one!" Then, trying to act calm and cool, Woody said, "Oh, yes— Andy's birthday party has been moved to today."

14

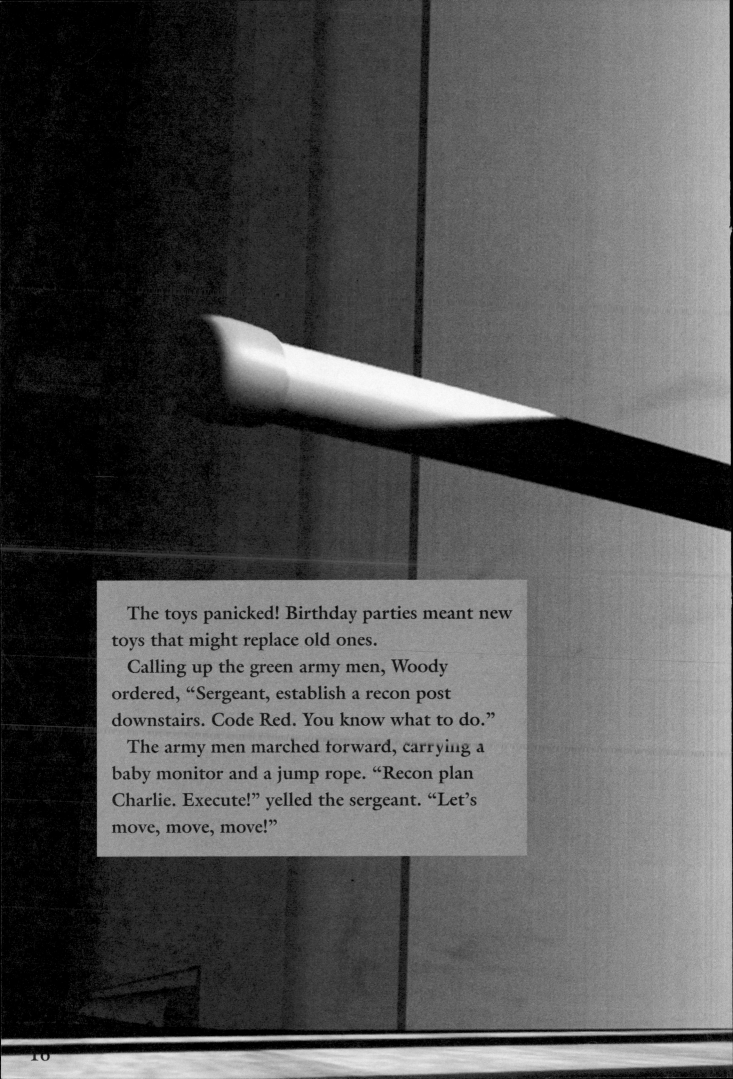

The toys panicked! Birthday parties meant new toys that might replace old ones.

Calling up the green army men, Woody ordered, "Sergeant, establish a recon post downstairs. Code Red. You know what to do."

The army men marched forward, carrying a baby monitor and a jump rope. "Recon plan Charlie. Execute!" yelled the sergeant. "Let's move, move, move!"

When the coast was clear, some of the army men slid down the jump rope, while others parachuted into the observation area. Setting up the baby monitor so they could communicate with Woody upstairs, the sergeant tried to get a read on the gift situation.

19

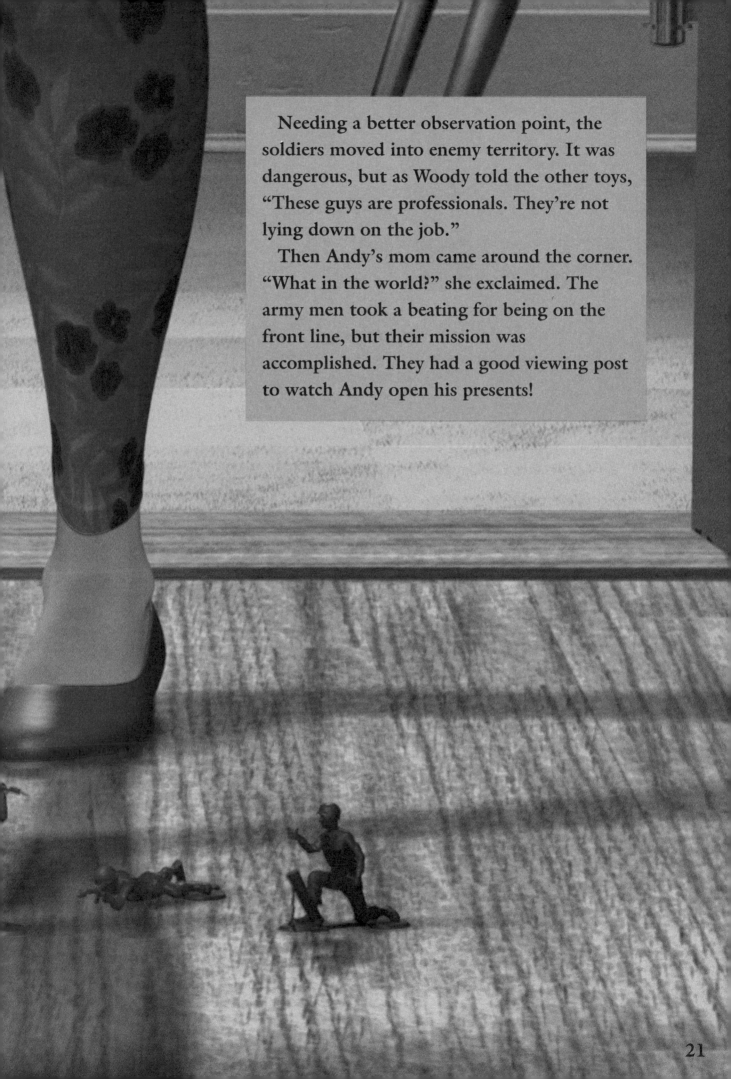

Needing a better observation point, the soldiers moved into enemy territory. It was dangerous, but as Woody told the other toys, "These guys are professionals. They're not lying down on the job."

Then Andy's mom came around the corner. "What in the world?" she exclaimed. The army men took a beating for being on the front line, but their mission was accomplished. They had a good viewing post to watch Andy open his presents!

Upstairs, the toys were waiting anxiously when they heard, "Come in, Mother Bird! This is Alpha Bravo."

"This is it!" yelled Woody.

The sergeant spoke again. "Andy's opening the first present now." The toys tensed. "The bow's coming off...he's ripping the wrapping paper...it's a...it's a lunchbox!" Everyone breathed a sigh of relief.

Andy got a lunchbox, bed sheets, and a board game—nothing to worry about, until...

"Come in, Mother Bird!" barked the sergeant. "Mom has pulled a surprise present from the closet. Andy's opening it..."

The air in Andy's room was thick with tension. Was this the gift that would spell a toy's doom? The sergeant's voice continued. "It's a huge package. I can't see...oh, it's...it's a..." But before he had time to report, the kids were flying up the stairs into Andy's room. The toys froze.

The next thing Woody knew, Andy and his friends had flung him to the floor to make room on his bed for...for what? Andy's mother called the boys back downstairs. They piled out of the room.

The toys came to life. Rex yelled up, "Woody? Who's up there with you?"

The toys were shocked when Woody crawled out from under the bed. "Woody, what are you doing there?" asked Slinky.

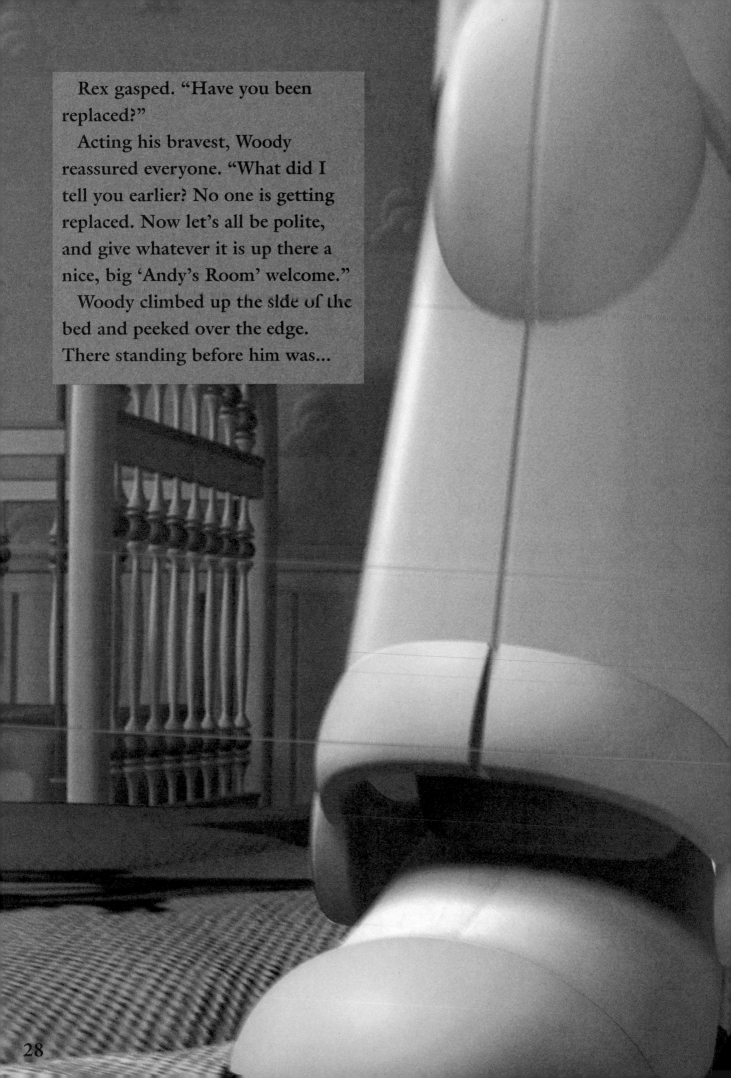

Rex gasped. "Have you been replaced?"

Acting his bravest, Woody reassured everyone. "What did I tell you earlier? No one is getting replaced. Now let's all be polite, and give whatever it is up there a nice, big 'Andy's Room' welcome."

Woody climbed up the side of the bed and peeked over the edge. There standing before him was...

...Buzz Lightyear, space ranger! Buzz didn't notice Woody at all. He was too busy trying to make contact with star command. "Star command—come in. Do you read me?"

Woody popped onto the scene, all smiles and friendly hellos. Never having seen a cowboy, Buzz reacted by taking a fighting stance. Woody tried to be his nicest. "Did I frighten you? Sorry. My name is Woody and this is Andy's room. There has been a bit of a mix-up. This is my spot, see, the bed here..."

Buzz checked out Woody's badge. "Local law enforcement. It's about time you got here. I'm Buzz Lightyear, space ranger, Universe Protection Unit. My ship has crash-landed here by mistake."

As the other toys came out to meet Buzz, he told them, "I am Buzz Lightyear. I come in peace." The other toys were very impressed. Buzz sported some very cool gadgets—a laser beam, wings, and karate-chop ability.

Woody had to defend his place as Andy's favorite toy. Trying to take back his position as leader, he told the others, "Look, we're all very impressed with Andy's new toy..."

Buzz couldn't believe his ears. "Toy?" he asked Woody.

"T-O-Y. Toy," said Woody.

"Excuse me. I think the term you're searching for is 'space ranger,'" said Buzz.

"He's not a space ranger!" Woody told the others.

"Yes, I am." said Buzz.

"Okay then," taunted Woody, "prove it."

Yelling "To infinity and beyond," Buzz leaped off the bed and glided across the room, then made a perfect landing.

Woody could see there was every chance Buzz would replace him as Andy's favorite toy. The other toys thought Buzz was the greatest!

All at once, they heard, "Help! Somebody help us!
We've got a man on a mine over here!" It was Sid,
Andy's neighbor, a cruel boy who tortured toys.
From the window, Andy's toys watched Sid blow a
toy soldier to smithereens.

"I could have stopped him," Buzz told the others.

"I would LOVE to see you try," Woody said, not
really meaning it at all.

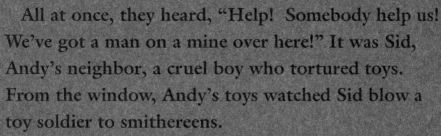

That evening, when Andy and his mom decided to go to Pizza Planet for dinner, only one toy could go along. Woody decided he would be that toy.

Woody sent RC, the remote-control car, toward Buzz, hoping to knock him behind the desk. But Buzz saw RC coming and jumped out of the way—only to fall out the window.

"BUZZ!" screamed the toys, looking down into the yard.

"Whirrr!! Whirrr-whirrr!!!" said RC. "This was no accident. Woody pushed Buzz."

The other toys turned on Woody. "Let's string him up by his pull-string," said Mr. Potato Head. It looked like curtains for Woody when Andy ran in, looking for Buzz.

He couldn't find Buzz, so Andy grabbed Woody. Woody was back in his number-one place again!

But just as Andy's car pulled out of the driveway, Buzz Lightyear grabbed onto the bumper. When the car stopped at a gas station and Andy and his mom got out, Buzz jumped in. He glared at Woody. "I want you to know that, even though you tried to terminate me, revenge is not an idea we promote on my planet."

"Oh, that's good," Woody said with relief.

"But we're not on my planet, are we?" Buzz attacked Woody. The two of them rolled over and over, until they fell out of the car. That was when Andy and his mom drove away, leaving Buzz and Woody stranded.

Buzz tried contacting Galactic Headquarters for help. Woody went ballistic! "YOU...ARE...A...TOY! You're an action figure! You are a child's plaything!"

But Buzz refused to believe him. Even after the two were able to make their way to Pizza Planet in a delivery truck, Buzz was still looking for a spaceship to take him home. And he found one—a rocket-shaped crane game filled with alien toys.

Buzz jumped in. "I am Buzz Lightyear," he told the aliens. "This is an intergalactic emergency!"

"Who's in charge here?" Buzz asked the aliens.

They pointed upward. "The cla-a-a-a-w! The claw is our master."

Knowing he could never show up back at Andy's without Buzz, Woody jumped into the game, too.

Then suddenly he heard, "Hey, Bozo!" It was Sid! Mean, scary, evil Sid was at the controls!

"Get down!" Woody yelled at Buzz. But it was too late.

"A Buzz Lightyear!" yelled Sid. "Yes!" Sid lowered the claw.

As Sid pulled Buzz up, Woody grabbed Buzz's legs and tried pulling Buzz down. He was just beginning to win when he heard, "He has been chosen. He must go." The aliens were helping Sid!

Suddenly Sid had Buzz and Woody in his grasp. "All right! Double prizes!" he yelled.

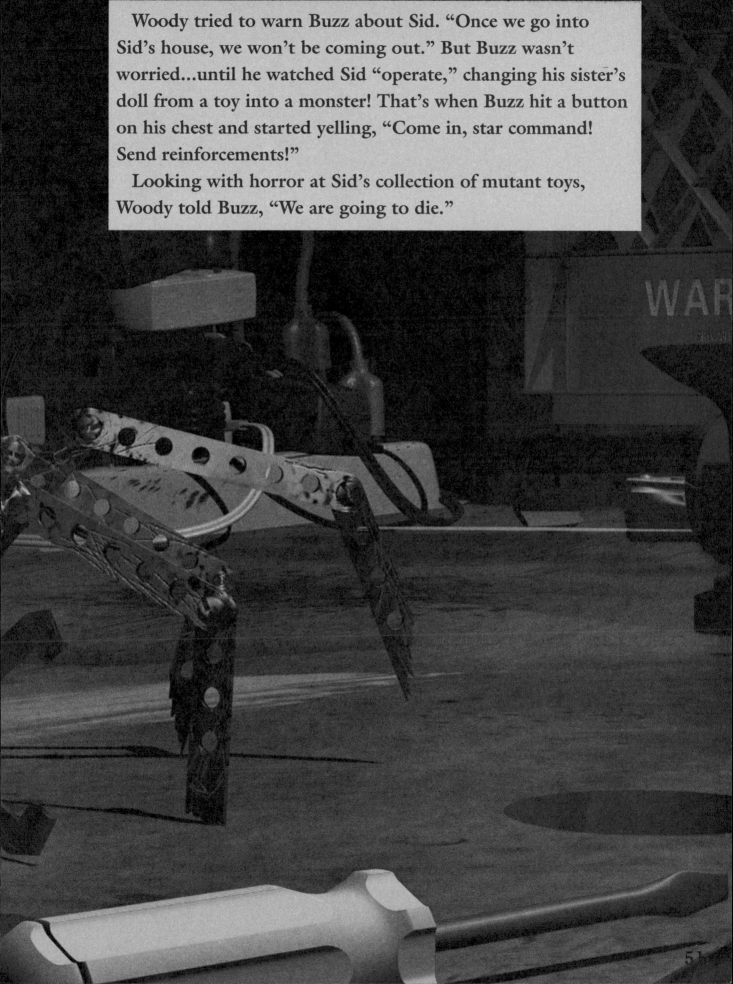

Woody tried to warn Buzz about Sid. "Once we go into Sid's house, we won't be coming out." But Buzz wasn't worried...until he watched Sid "operate," changing his sister's doll from a toy into a monster! That's when Buzz hit a button on his chest and started yelling, "Come in, star command! Send reinforcements!"

Looking with horror at Sid's collection of mutant toys, Woody told Buzz, "We are going to die."

Woody might have been right. They were saved from disaster only by Sid's mom yelling, "Sid! Your snacks are ready!"

When Sid left, Woody yelled, "The door! It's open!" They slipped out of Sid's room and started down the hallway. Seeing Sid's dog, Scud, sleeping on the landing, Buzz clapped his hand over Woody's mouth for silence. "Split up!" he hissed.

Woody ran into a closet, but Buzz heard star command calling him
at last. Delighted, he made his way toward the sound. "Calling Buzz
Lightyear! Come in, Buzz Lightyear! This is star command!"

Buzz was ecstatic—until he also heard the TV announcer say, "Yes,
kids, Buzz Lightyear. The world's greatest superhero is now the
world's greatest toy!" Woody was right. Buzz was just a toy.

Heartbroken, Buzz tried to prove the TV commercial wrong. He
made his way up the stairs and tried to fly! He fell flat on his back and
broke off his arm. That's when Sid's sister, Hannah, found him and
invited him to a tea party for her dolls.

When Hannah left her room, Woody raced in to save Buzz. But Buzz had lost heart. "I'm a sham!" Buzz told Woody. "Look at me! I can't even fly!" Now that he knew he was only a toy, Buzz could see no reason to go on living.

But Woody wanted out of Sid's house...now!

And he wasn't leaving without Buzz.

Making his way to the window in Sid's room, Woody called out, "Hey, guys! Hey!" Across the way in Andy's room, Mr. Potato Head yelled to the other toys, "It's Woody!"

All the toys rushed to the window. "What are you doing over there?" asked Bo Peep.

"It's a long story, Bo. I'll explain later," said Woody. Then he threw a string of Christmas lights over toward Andy's window and yelled, "Here, catch this!"

Slinky caught it! For one moment, Woody thought he and Buzz would make it back to Andy's house. But then Mr. Potato Head threw the lights back, saying, "Have you all forgotten what he did to Buzz?"

That left Woody and Buzz at Sid's mercy. Rushing into his room with a big box, Sid pulled out a rocket. "What am I gonna blow?" he asked. "Hey, where's that wimpy cowboy doll?"

Woody hid, but Buzz no longer cared about anything. He let himself fall into Sid's clutches.

Strapping Buzz to the rocket, Sid yelled, "TO INFINITY AND BEYOND!" He was about to take Buzz to the backyard and send him into the stratosphere when it started to rain.

"Sid Phillips reporting. Launch of the shuttle has been delayed due to adverse weather conditions. Tomorrow's forecast: sunny."

That night, while Sid slept, Woody pleaded for Buzz's help. He was trapped underneath a milk crate. "Buzz, I can't do this without you. I need your help."

But Buzz was too depressed to react. "I can't help. I can't help anyone."

Woody couldn't stand this way of thinking. "Over in that house is a kid who thinks you are the greatest," he told Buzz. "And it's not because you're a space ranger, pal, it's because you're a TOY! You are HIS toy."

Suddenly the milk crate began to shake. "Come on, Sheriff," said Buzz. "There's a kid over in that house who needs us. Now let's get you out of this thing."

Just as Buzz got Woody free, Sid's alarm went BRRI-I-I-NG!

Sid jumped out of bed, grabbed Buzz, and went outside to shoot him to infinity and beyond.

Woody was at a loss. How could he help Buzz? Then he remembered Sid's mutant toys. Coaxing them out from under Sid's bed, he told them, "There's a good toy down there and he's gonna be blown to bits in a few minutes. We've gotta save him—but I need your help."

The mutant toys and Woody made their way past Scud to Sid's backyard. The mutants took their prearranged battle stations, and Woody made his way towards Buzz. "Everything's under control," Woody told him. Then Woody lay down on the grass and froze.

"Houston, all systems are go," said Sid, coming out of the toolhouse. Then he saw Woody. "How'd you get out here?" he asked, picking him up. He tucked a match in Woody's holster and threw him into the barbecue. "You and I can have a cookout later," Sid sneered.

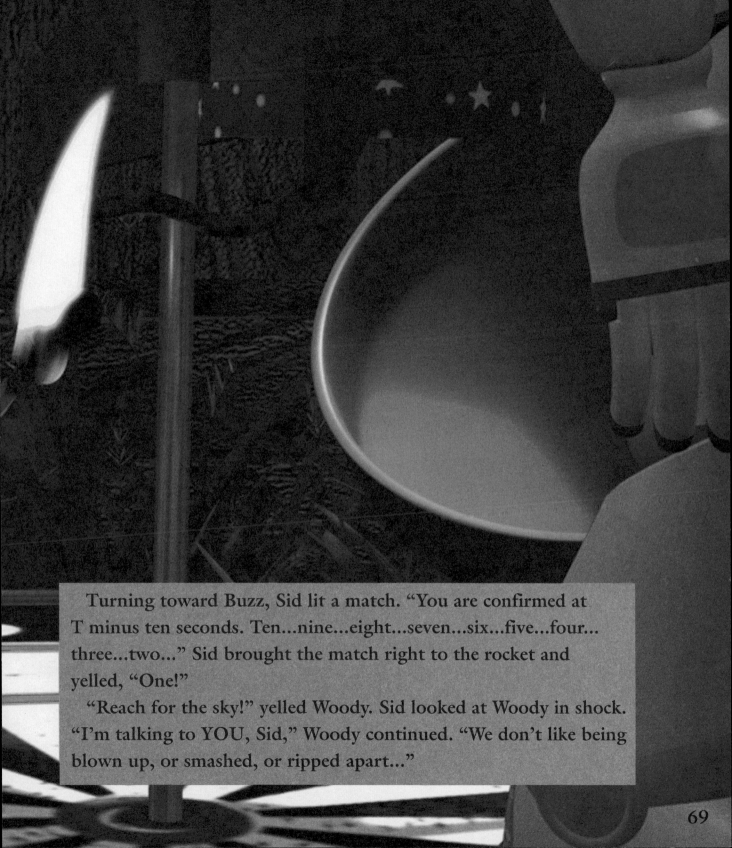

Turning toward Buzz, Sid lit a match. "You are confirmed at T minus ten seconds. Ten...nine...eight...seven...six...five...four... three...two..." Sid brought the match right to the rocket and yelled, "One!"

"Reach for the sky!" yelled Woody. Sid looked at Woody in shock. "I'm talking to YOU, Sid," Woody continued. "We don't like being blown up, or smashed, or ripped apart..."

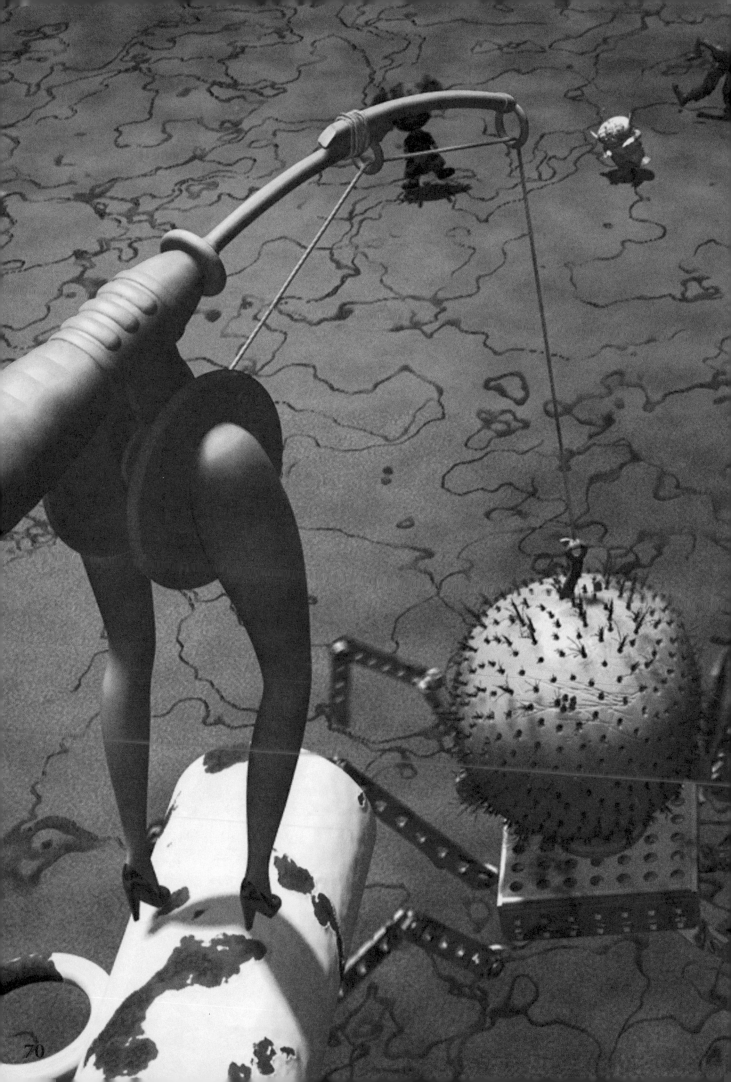

"W-w-w-we?" Sid asked weakly.
"That's right," said Woody. "Your toys."
Suddenly Sid's mutant toys rose up from around the yard.

One by one, they started marching towards him. Grabbing at him. Taunting him. Sid had only one reaction. "AAAAAAAAAAAAAGGGGGGGHHHHH!" he screamed as he ran into the house.

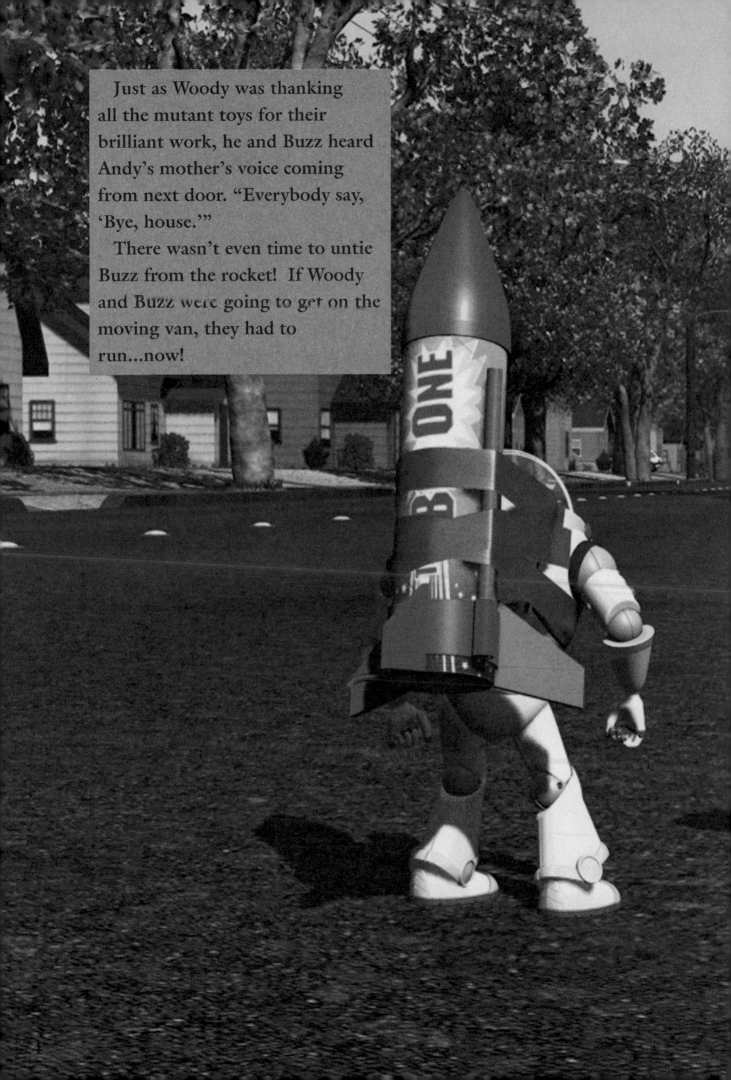

Just as Woody was thanking all the mutant toys for their brilliant work, he and Buzz heard Andy's mother's voice coming from next door. "Everybody say, 'Bye, house.'"

There wasn't even time to untie Buzz from the rocket! If Woody and Buzz were going to get on the moving van, they had to run...now!

The two of them ran to catch up with the van. Buzz grabbed onto a chain dangling from the back of the van and hauled himself up. Then it was Woody's turn.

He'd almost made it when Scud made a lunge for him. Woody was trapped between the van and the dog. But Buzz came to the rescue! Jumping onto Scud's nose, he stopped the dog in his tracks.

Now there was only one little problem. Woody was safely on the van, but Buzz was lying in the street.

Entering the van, Woody made his way to the box labeled ANDY'S TOYS—KEEP OUT! Opening it, he grabbed RC, the remote-control car, and aimed it towards Buzz.

Still convinced that Woody was up to no good, the other toys attacked. "Toss him overboard," ordered Mr. Potato Head.

Luckily for Woody, RC and Buzz whizzed by and picked him up before any cars could smash him.

"Thanks for the ride," a relieved Woody told them. "Now let's catch up to that truck!"

Back on the van, Lenny, the toy binoculars, suddenly spotted Buzz and Woody. "Guys! Guys!" he told the other toys. "Woody's riding RC...and Buzz is with him."

"It is Buzz!" said Bo Peep. "Woody was telling the truth."

Feeling terrible for doubting Woody, the toys were determined to help. Rocky, the toy strongman, lowered a ramp, but it was too late. RC's batteries were running out. As the van pulled away, RC sputtered to a stop.

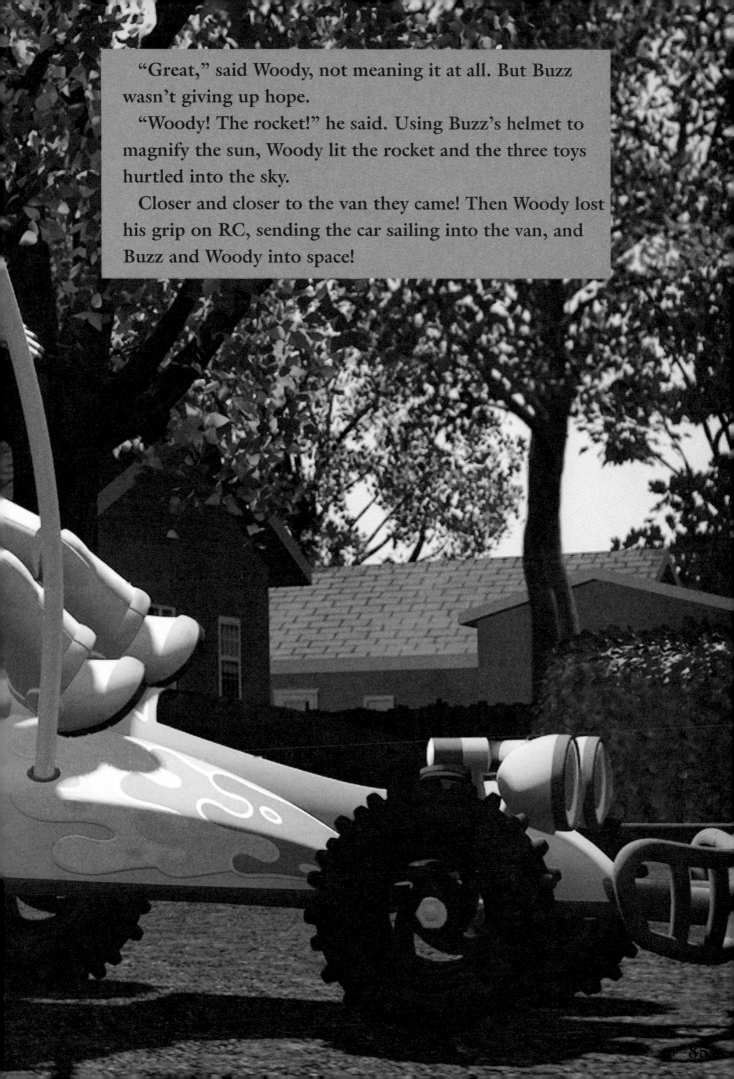

"Great," said Woody, not meaning it at all. But Buzz wasn't giving up hope.

"Woody! The rocket!" he said. Using Buzz's helmet to magnify the sun, Woody lit the rocket and the three toys hurtled into the sky.

Closer and closer to the van they came! Then Woody lost his grip on RC, sending the car sailing into the van, and Buzz and Woody into space!

"Hey, Buzz! You're flying!" Woody cried.

"Technically, I'm gliding," said Buzz. "But let's not spoil the moment."

And so the two friends hurtled through the sky, with Woody yelling, "To infinity and beyond!"

Then he looked down to see something a little frightening.

"Uh, Buzz?!" he said. "We missed the truck!"

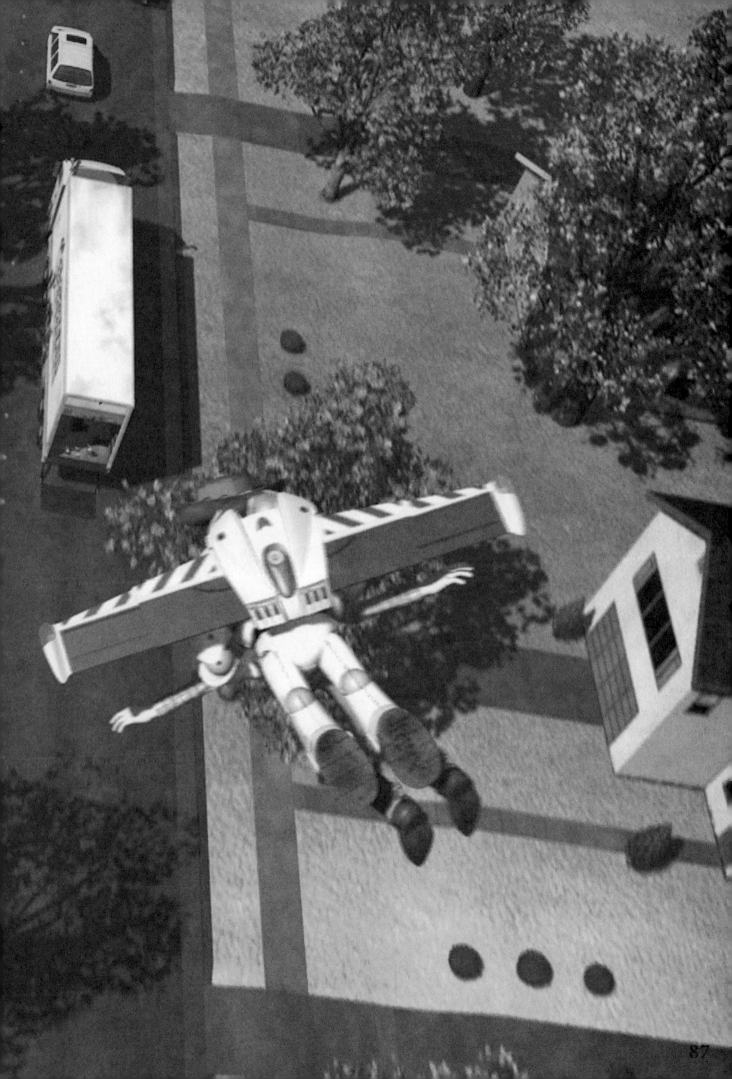

"We're not aiming for the truck!" cried Buzz. Making a graceful loop, Buzz headed for the sunroof of Andy's car. He executed a perfect dive into a box on the seat next to Andy.

"Hey! Wow!" yelled Andy with glee. "Woody! Buzz!"

"Where were they?" his mother asked.

"Here. In the car," said Andy.

A few months later, on Christmas morning in Andy's new house, the toys were listening to the baby monitor once again.

"Frankincense—this is Myrrh. Come in," said the toy army sergeant from his command post downstairs.

Afraid once again of being replaced by a new toy,
everyone listened closely, except Woody and Bo Peep.
"Merry Christmas, Sheriff," Bo Peep whispered.

Suddenly the sergeant spoke again. "Molly's first present is...Mrs. Potato Head."

"Way to go!" Hamm told Mr. Potato Head, who was beside himself with excitement.

"Come in, Frankincense," boomed the sergeant on the baby monitor. "Andy is now opening his present...larger box...can't see..." Static cut the sergeant off.

Buzz banged the monitor. "Buzz, you aren't worried, are you?" teased Woody.

"Me? No, no," said Buzz. "No. Are you?"

"Now, Buzz," laughed Woody. "What can Andy possibly get that is worse than you?"

Then over the baby monitor came the sound of a bark. "Wow! A puppy!" yelled Andy.